Samuel French Acting Edition

Deep in the Heart of Tuna

by Jaston Williams,
Joe Sears & Ed Howard

‖SAMUEL FRENCH‖

SAMUELFRENCH.COM   **SAMUELFRENCH.CO.UK**

MUSIC USE NOTE

Licensees are solely responsible for obtaining formal written permission from copyright owners to use copyrighted music in the performance of this play and are strongly cautioned to do so. If no such permission is obtained by the licensee, then the licensee must use only original music that the licensee owns and controls. Licensees are solely responsible and liable for all music clearances and shall indemnify the copyright owners of the play(s) and their licensing agent, Samuel French, against any costs, expenses, losses and liabilities arising from the use of music by licensees. Please contact the appropriate music licensing authority in your territory for the rights to any incidental music.

IMPORTANT BILLING AND CREDIT REQUIREMENTS

If you have obtained performance rights to this title, please refer to your licensing agreement for important billing and credit requirements.

DEEP IN THE HEART OF TUNA was first produced under the title *TUNA'S GREATEST HITS* by Tuna Does Vegas, LLC at the Charles W. Eisemann Center in Richardson, Texas on February 12, 2012. The performance was directed by Ed Howard, with sets by Christopher McCollum, costumes by Linda Fisher, and sound by Ken Huncovsky. The production stage manager was Tyler Fannon, and the assistant stage manager was Tristan Ludden. Wardrobe supervisors were Patricia Hawkins and Karen Aydelotle-Jones. The cast was as follows:

ARLES, DIDI, JODY, CHAD, PETEY & VERA.............. Jaston Williams

THURSTON, BERTHA, YIPPY, PEARL & REVEREND SPIKES ...... Joe Sears

CHARACTERS

ARLES STRUVIE – Tuna's celebrity DJ

THURSTON WHEELIS – Arles' partner DJ

DIDI SNAVELY – owner of Didi's Used Weapons

BERTHA BUMILLER – beleaguered Tuna housewife

JODY BUMILLER – Bertha's son with a dog addiction

CHAD HARTFORD – a reporter from Houston

PETEY FISK – the sole member of the Tuna Humane Society

YIPPY – a small, obnoxious dog

PEARL BURRAS – Bertha's Aunt, a notorious chicken farmer

VERA CARP – vice president of the Smut Snatchers of the New Order

REVEREND SPIKES – president of the Smut Snatchers of the New Order

AUTHORS' NOTES

Deep in the Heart of Tuna is the story of the romance between bewildered housewife Bertha Bumiller and local DJ Arles Struvie, a story told over the decades in the four *Tuna* plays set in Texas' third-smallest town. Though written to accommodate two actors making quick changes and taking on all the roles, the play can be performed with a cast as large as eleven. If done with a larger cast, it may be possible to present live the dialogue marked in the script as "on tape." The play was written to incorporate mime into the action. The only object not mimed was the tabloid magazine that Bertha reads while portraying Yippy, but the producer may choose to use actual props.

ACT I

Scene One: Radio Station OKKK
After Labor Day ~ 1980s

(Onstage are two kitchen tables, four chairs, and a console radio equipped with a speaker and interior light source. We hear Texas music* in the house and ending over the radio. Lights fade to radio; we hear a test tone, then **ARLES** *on tape.)*

ARLES. *(On tape.)* This is Radio Station OKKK in Tuna, Texas, serving the Greater Tuna area at two hundred and seventy-five watts signing on.

(Lights up to reveal **THURSTON WHEELIS** *and* **ARLES STRUVIE.***)*

THURSTON. Good morning, Tuna, this is Thurston Wheelis.

ARLES. And this is Arles Struvie.

THURSTON. And this is the Wheelis...

ARLES. Struvie...

THURSTON. Report.

ARLES. And here we go with the news. Take it away, Thurston.

THURSTON. Well, folks, in the news today, we've got the winner of the Tuna Junior High American Heritage Essay Contest for this year. And this year's winner is Connie Carp. She's the daughter of W.H. and Vera Carp here in Tuna, and the name of her essay was titled

---

*A license to produce *Deep in the Heart of Tuna* does not include a performance license for any third-party or copyrighted music. Licensees should create an original composition or use music in the public domain. For further information, please see Music Use Note on page 3.

"Human Rights, Why Bother?" Second place went to Jimbo Beaumont for "Living with Radiation," and third place went to Levita Posey for her essay titled, "The Other Side of Bigotry." I'll tell you, Arles, with subjects like that, I don't know how they ever picked a winner.

ARLES. I don't either. I tell you, it should make the citizens of Tuna proud to know that we're still producing well-educated students who know what America is all about.

THURSTON. They do.

ARLES. They do. They do. They do.

> (**ARLES** *gets a note handed to him by Ronnie, an imaginary office assistant.*)

ARLES.	**THURSTON.**
Thank you, Ronnie.	They do. I always thought
This just in.	they did a fine job
Excuse me, Thurston.	
	Go right ahead.

ARLES. Oh, I have bad news for the Greater Tuna area. Former County Judge Roscoe Buckner died at his home yesterday; he had suffered a severe stroke. Buckner, who was judge in the Greater Tuna area for forty-seven years and who hung more people in the thirties than any other active judge, had a history of heart trouble. Now, the body will lie in state at Hubert Funeral Home, starting today at twelve noon, and Wexler Hubert says if you come before noon you're gonna have to wait, 'cause the judge won't be ready till noon.

THURSTON. Well, I tell ya, folks, that's some bad news.

ARLES. It is.

THURSTON. It is.

ARLES. It is. It is. Now on the Art scene, the on-again, off-again auditions for the Tuna Little Theatre production of *My Fair Lady* are on again. Now, they'd been called off due to a lack of budget. But Joe Bob Lipsey, who is the director of the show this year, and who is a recent graduate of Southwest Texas Eastern A and I State University, said that he found a way to go ahead with the production by using sets and costumes from last year's show of *South Pacific*, and according to Joe Bob, this is gonna be the first production ever of *My Fair Lady* set in Polynesia.

THURSTON. Well, Arles you never know, something like that's just li'ble to put us on the map.

ARLES. On it.

ARLES.	**THURSTON.**
On it. On it. On it. Well, Thurston, you got that farm report?	On it. They'll find us.

(ARLES exits and changes to DIDI.)

THURSTON. Oh yeah, it's around here someplace...
(Searching for the farm report.) I don't know where the damn thing is! Ronnie?! Well, I hate it when I have to make it up. I know that cantaloupes were higher than a city skirt the other day. There's something we're not supposed to eat. Well hell, here it is! Looks like beef up, pork down, chickens vacillatin', and there's not a thing on here about sow bellies. So let's just go to a commercial from our sponsor, Didi Snavely, of Didi's Used Weapons. Didi!

(Lights come up on DIDI's spot. THURSTON exits, changes to BERTHA. DIDI enters.)

DIDI. Does the high cost of security have you blue? If so, come by the store and browse through our complete selection of used guns and knives, or find what you need in our mace and tear gas department. Now we understand that many people are hesitant to buy used weapons, but all of Didi's weapons are absolutely guaranteed to kill. Now if you find a weapon here that won't kill, you bring it back, and we'll give you something that will. It's on our guarantee: "If Didi's can't kill it, it's immortal."

Scene Two: Bertha's Kitchen

> (DIDI *exits, changes to* JODY. *Melancholy Texas music* plays in house, then fades to radio. Lights fade to radio, then come up on Bertha's kitchen. We hear* BERTHA *off.)*

BERTHA. *(Offstage.)* Charlene! Stanley! Don't make me call you again.

> (BERTHA *enters wearing a fall-themed blouse and turns off the radio.)*

Jody, honey, get in here and finish your breakfast.

> (JODY *enters through an imaginary screen door.)*

Jody, honey, you want some more oatmeal?

JODY. No, Mama.

BERTHA. How 'bout some of these biscuits and gravy; Honey, you hardly even touched 'em.

JODY. I already had some, Mama.

BERTHA. Well, baby, I could fry you some more bacon.

JODY. Mama, I don't want nothin'.

BERTHA. Is there something wrong with them hash browns?

JODY. No, Mama.

BERTHA. Well, have some more... Jody what's that out there on the back porch? Oh, no! No, Jody, you didn't. Uh-uh! I will not have another puppy!

JODY. Mama, it followed me home.

BERTHA. From where?

JODY. From Petey Fisk.

BERTHA. That Petey Fisk has given you another dog. He saves the dogs of the world and sends them home for me to feed. Well, you can't have another dog. Eight

---

*A license to produce *Deep in the Heart of Tuna* does not include a performance license for any third-party or copyrighted music. Licensees should create an original composition or use music in the public domain. For further information, please see Music Use Note on page 3.

dogs is too many. You cannot have another dog, Little Jody.

JODY. I'll take care of it, Mama.

BERTHA. Honey, it's not a matter of taking care of it. It's not normal. It's not normal for you to have eight to ten dogs followin' you all the time, and don't let that dog in the house. That reporter from Houston will be here any minute.

> (**JODY** *exits through the screen door, letting the puppy in, and changes to* **CHAD.**)

I said, don't let that... Now isn't that the cutest little thing... Awwoohhh, get down. Quit. Stop it... He's done it to me again. He has done it to me again. Come on, you. Yes, you... Come on and get out there with the rest of 'em. I gotta set for an interview.

(To the other dogs.) Get away from that door! All of you! Get Back!

> *(She lets the puppy out.)*

Now come on, you. You sweet thing... Now y'all let her alone. Bless her heart, isn't she cute? ...I could kill that goddamn Petey Fisk.

> *(Doorbell.)*

Oh, it's that reporter from Houston. Coming!

> *(She checks her appearance.)*

> *(Doorbell.)*

I said I was coming.

> *(Doorbell.)*

Well, you'll just have to hold onto your horses! I said I was coming.

> *(Doorbell.)*

Yes?

> (**CHAD** *enters.*)

CHAD. Mrs. Bumiller?

BERTHA. Yes.

CHAD. My name is Chad Hartford.

BERTHA. Oh, come in, Mr. Hartford. Could I get you something to drink? A cup of coffee?

CHAD. I don't care for anything to drink. I'm in a bit of a hurry. Could we get right to the interview?

BERTHA. Well, certainly.

CHAD. Now, you are chairing the Censorship of the Text Books Committee, am I right?

BERTHA. Oh, no no no no. That's the Reverend Spikes who heads that committee...although I am a member. We're gonna have a meetin' this afternoon, by the way. But please don't come. The Reverend Spikes, he just hates the press. I think it's because of all those old-folks' homes he owns, and all them terrible things they said about him in the newspapers. Well, I better shut up. Anyway, I head the subcommittee that wants to snatch the books off the shelves of the local high school library. Some of those books are absolutely disgusting. Our children have no business reading them, and somebody has got to protect the minds of the children.

CHAD. Before we get to the books, Mrs. Bumiller, could you tell me what in your background do you feel qualifies you to censor library books?

BERTHA. Well, I can briefly list my activities, if you like.

CHAD. Please.

BERTHA. Well, I'm currently president of the Ladies for a Better Tuna. I am den mother for Den 225. I'm the only high-C soprano in the First Baptist Choir. And I'm currently recorder of the Havelina Club. That's a women's auxiliary of the Wild Hogs. It's kind of a break-off of the Lions Club. We just thought the Lions were too liberal. I'm the former head of the local B.B.B. That's the Better Baptist Bureau. And I'm a member of our shut-in visiting squad, the Tuna Helpers. And I'm currently president and co-founder of Citizens for Fewer Blacks in Literature...

CHAD. Thank you, Mrs. Bumiller. I think I get the idea. Now, exactly what are the books that you think should be removed from the shelves?

BERTHA. Well, now there's four of 'em that we're gonna try and have removed nationwide. And then we're gonna go from there.

CHAD. What are the four books, Mrs. Bumiller?

BERTHA. *Roots*. Now, we don't deny that *Roots* has been a very popular TV series, but we feel it only shows one side of the slavery issue.

CHAD. Go on.

BERTHA. *Bury My Heart at Wounded Knee*. Well, it's the most disgusting title to begin with; it just makes me want to erp. That book vilifies a great American, General Custer. And it encourages the reader to believe that the United States Government can't be trusted in makin' any treaties.

CHAD. What's next?

BERTHA. *Huckleberry Finn*, by Mark Twain.

CHAD. Did he write that?

BERTHA. Un-huh. Now, that book shows a pre-teenage boy avoidin' his chores, runnin' away from home, cohortin' with a Negro convict, and puttin' on women's clothes.

CHAD. Go on.

BERTHA. *Romeo and Juliet*.

CHAD. What, pray tell, is wrong with *Romeo and Juliet*?

BERTHA. It just shows sex among teenagers, that's all. And we're not for that, and we're certainly not going to encourage it. Besides, it shows a rampant disrespect for parental authority.

CHAD. You are aware that William Shakespeare wrote that play?

BERTHA. Oh, yes we are. And we're lookin' into the rest of his stuff too. He wrote *Barefoot in the Park*, didn't he?

CHAD. Mrs. Bumiller, quite often these days, people claim to talk to God. Do you talk to God?

BERTHA. Well, I pray.

CHAD. I didn't ask you that, Mrs. Bumiller. I asked if you talk to God directly.

BERTHA. Well, no, I don't. But he leaves little messages for me...with the Reverend Spikes. And second-hand messages from the Lord is good enough for me.

CHAD. Thank you, Mrs. Bumiller. I think we've got one hell of a story here.

BERTHA. Don't you rush off. I've got other interesting things to tell you about Tuna.

CHAD. Well, I'm sure it just boggles the mind, Mrs. Bumiller, but I really must run.

BERTHA. Now, wait a minute. What was the name of your magazine?

CHAD. *Intellect.*

BERTHA. I don't believe we have that here in Tuna.

CHAD. I'll see that you get a copy. Goodbye, Mrs. Bumiller.

(**CHAD** *exits and changes to* **PETEY**.)

BERTHA. Well, bye.

(*To herself.*) I think reporters ask the silliest questions. Well, I guess I'm lucky he didn't ask more than he did. Thank God he didn't ask me about my family. Poor Charlene, that girl, she's just going crazy over not getting cheerleader. I said, "Charlene, honey, settle down, it'll be fine. You'll get cheerleader next year." And she looks at me with tears streaming down her cheeks and says, "Mama, I'm a senior." I don't know how to tell my only daughter she's never gonna be a cheerleader. I just don't know how to do it. Oooohhh, and Stanley. I swear I don't know what I'm gonna do with that boy, datin' that Mexican girl. He never has been right. Oh, but Jody's going to be okay, except that he's got eight to ten dogs following him all the time, but he'll grow out of that. I know he will. I hope. At least I didn't have to lie about Hank. I swear I've cooked and cleaned for that sorry son-of-a-bitch for twenty-seven years, and he won't even take me to the drive-in movies. Of course, I pretend not to notice as we go to church on Sunday morning, after Saturday night. After I've smelled the perfume and seen the lipstick smears. I swear, sometimes I just wish that man would have a stroke! I swear I do! ...I don't mean that... God, forgive me. I don't mean that. I'm so glad that reporter didn't ask.

> (**BERTHA** *turns on radio, takes out* Enquirer, *sits to read. We hear the end of the melancholy Texas music that was at the scene's beginning.**
> **PETEY** *enters.*)

PETEY. This is Petey Fisk, speaking to you for the Greater Tuna Humane Society.

BERTHA AS YIPPY. Yip. Yip.

PETEY. I'm here to introduce this week's pet-of-the-week.

BERTHA AS YIPPY. Yip. Yip. Yip.

PETEY. His name is Yippy-yi-yi-yeh.

BERTHA AS YIPPY. Yip. Yip.

PETEY. But we just call him Yippy.

BERTHA AS YIPPY. Yip. Yip. Yip.

PETEY. That's why.

BERTHA AS YIPPY. Yip. Yip. Yip.

PETEY. This is Yippy's fifth appearance as pet-of-the-week...

BERTHA AS YIPPY. Yip. Yip. Yip.

PETEY. And this charming little part-rat terrier, part-Chihuahua will make a lovely pet for someone.

BERTHA AS YIPPY. Yip.

PETEY. We're sure.

BERTHA AS YIPPY. Yip. Yip. Yip.

PETEY. Stop it! His only real drawback as a pet is a tendency to hyperactive behavior.

BERTHA AS YIPPY. Yip. Yip. Yip. Yip. Yip. Yip.

PETEY. Stop it! As you can understand, we here at the Humane Society quite often have trouble giving away small, shrill animals.

BERTHA AS YIPPY. Yip. Yip. Yip.

PETEY. But we still have hope for Yippy.

BERTHA AS YIPPY. Yip. Yip.

PETEY. We know there must be some deaf person out there who would love to have a dog, and who would make the perfect owner for Yippy. Now, if there's any deaf person out there listening who wants this dog, please, call me, Petey Fisk, at 477-7777.

BERTHA AS YIPPY. Yip. Yip. Yip. Yip.

PETEY. Call anytime, day or night.

BERTHA AS YIPPY. Yip. Yip.

PETEY. Please call!

BERTHA AS YIPPY. Yip. Yip.

PETEY. If you're out of town, call collect.

BERTHA AS YIPPY. Yip. Yip. Yip.

PETEY. I gotta get rid of this dog!

BERTHA AS YIPPY. Yip. Yip.

PETEY. This is Petey Fisk, speaking to you for the Greater Tuna Humane Society.

BERTHA AS YIPPY. Yip. Yip.

PETEY. Thank you.

BERTHA AS YIPPY. Yip. Yip. Yip. Yip.

> (**PETEY** *exits.* **BERTHA** *turns off radio, gets phone, and dials. The phone rings once from her perspective and once from* **PETEY***'s.* **PETEY** *re-enters and answers phone.*)

PETEY. Hello.

BERTHA. Hello, Petey? Is this Petey Fisk?

PETEY. Yes.

BERTHA. This is Bertha Bumiller, Petey, and I wanna talk to you, and I want you to listen. Do you understand, Petey?

PETEY. What're you talkin'...

BERTHA. I said I wanna talk and I want you to listen. Petey, I have tried to think what I have done to deserve this life I lead, a husband who spent four years in prison for robbin' a fillin' station of forty-seven dollars. And there are my psycho twins, Charlene and Stanley, who you know have caused me no end of grief. And my youngest, Jody, is never seen that he doesn't have a pack of dogs around him. They follow him to school. They follow him home. They follow him everywhere. And last week, Petey, I nearly had to whup him because he wanted to take 'em to the First Baptist Church!

PETEY. Well, now, Bertha...

BERTHA. I said, I talk and you listen. Now, Petey, we have a very serious situation on our hands. My son Jody has something as bad as a drug habit. Jody has a dog habit. He has a psychological addiction to those dogs, and you, Petey Fisk, you're a puppy pusher!

PETEY. Well, I never...

BERTHA. I said I talk and you listen! Now, I will put up with Shep, Woffie, Trixie, Bingo, Blossom, Sweet Nothin', Dolly and Thunder, but if that little Yippy half-rat, half-Chihuahua, half-whatever that you been talkin' about on the radio...if that dog shows up at my house, Petey Fisk, they'll have to drag the river to find your body!

PETEY. But I... I...

BERTHA. I said listen! Now, Petey, I'm gonna call my Aunt Pearl Burras... I swear to God, I'm gonna call my Aunt Pearl, and I'm gonna tell her to make up a whole batch of her bitter pills. I mean business. I'm as serious as a stroke. I will not be the mother of an addict, whether he's on opium or basset hounds. Now say goodbye, Petey.

> (**BERTHA** *hangs up, exits in a huff, and changes to* **PEARL.**)

PETEY. *(After a long pause.)* Goodbye.

> (**PETEY** *gets out a pen and paper and begins to write a letter.*)

Scene Three: Aunt Pearl's Backyard

PETEY. Mrs. Pearl Burras, General Delivery, Tuna Texas. Dear Mrs. Burras. After a recent unsettling phone call from your niece Bertha Bumiller, I feel compelled to write to you. As you know, relations have never been strong between the Humane Society and those who raise chickens. We do understand that this is your livelihood, disgusting as it may be to those of us here at the Humane Society.

> *(Lights come up on Pearl's backyard.* **PEARL** *enters.)*

PEARL. *(Feeding chickens.)* Here chick, chick, chick, chickie. Come and get it babies. Eat it up, eat it up. Babies, babies, babies...

PETEY. We do feel, however, that you are posing a danger to the children of your neighborhood, as well as their pets. We're sure you love the kids of your neighborhood as much as we do.

PEARL. *(Spotting children in her yard.)* Get out of those tomatoes! Get out of 'em! I'm gonna call Sheriff Givens! Let me at 'em.

PETEY. Mrs. Burras, we have traced over seventy dog poisonings to your doorstep. Now, don't you think you've taken eccentricity a bit too far?

PEARL. Oh, they've left that poodle in my yard. I'll bet it's an egg-sucker! Where is it?

PETEY. We feel that you have been somewhat over-zealous in the protection of your chickens.

PEARL. Where's my strychnine? Please to God, don't tell me I'm out!

PETEY. In fact, Mrs. Burras, there are those of us at the Humane Society who believe that you actually enjoy poisoning dogs.

PEARL. I'll kill Henry if he's hidden my strychnine!

PETEY. We are well aware of your "bitter pills," those strychnine-laced biscuits rolled into enticing little dough balls.

PEARL. Oh, I found it. Henry thought he'd be smart and hide it, but I found it. I'm gonna kill me a poodle. Now, where's my biscuits? I'm gonna make you a bitter pill.

PETEY. We are also aware that your husband Henry is the owner of Ripper, the finest bird dog in Dewey County. How could anybody who lives around a $2,000 dog like Ripper poison people's puppies so heartlessly?

PEARL. Here puppy, puppy, puppy. Get over here egglips. Come here and get the bitter pill... Get back, Ripper! It's not for you. You stay back! Get back; it's not for you, Ripper... Oh, I didn't mean to scare you; now come on. I'll set it down right here, and you come and get it... Ripper! Don't eat that! Oh my God, Ripper's eaten the bitter pill!

PETEY. Mrs. Burras, you have classic symptoms of canicidal thumbitus, a psychological disorder that causes you to want to kill other people's dogs, for real or imagined reasons.

PEARL. Oh my God, I've poisoned Henry's bird dog... Oh, look at him shake.

PETEY. Now the only known cure for canicidal thumbitus is to surround the patient with lots and lots of dogs until the urge to kill passes.

PEARL. Oh, what am I going to do? Oh, think Pearl, think. Think think think. Oh, I know what I'll do. I know what I'll do! I'll call Stanley: I'll have him come over here and drag that dog out in the road. We'll run over it with the Pontiac. We'll tell Henry it got hit by a car.

PETEY. And are you in luck, Mrs. Burras. The Humane Society has a one-way bus ticket for you to Dallas, to the Texas State Dog Fair, where you can be surrounded by over four thousand dogs.

PEARL. *(Dialing phone.)* That's what I'll do. I'll call Stanley. I can count on Stanley.

PETEY. Mrs. Burras, if you make it through the entire show without poisoning a single animal, the Humane Society will pay your bus fare home. Think, you can find peace of mind, and the dogs of your neighborhood can have a respite from the death and carnage to which they have been subjected. Sincerely, Petey Fisk, Greater Tuna Humane Society.

(**PETEY** *exits and changes to* **VERA**.)

PEARL. Hello Stanley, this is Pearl. Get over here quick, I need you... I want you to run over Henry's bird dog... Ripper... Umhmm... Well, he's already dead... I killed him... Oh, Stanley, I know it's not as much fun running over a dead dog! But please to God, get over here, I don't believe I can stand it... You're a good nephew... I'll see you in a minute... All right. Goodbye. (*Hangs up.*) Oh, I knew I could count on Stanley. Oh, and while he's here, I'll get him to run me down to the funeral parlor so I can view Judge Buckner, oh Lord, nothing would get me out in this heat except to see him dead. I just want to see for myself. Make for sure.

(**PEARL** *exits. Lights fade to radio and we hear* **THURSTON** *and* **ARLES** *on tape.*)

ARLES. (*On tape.*) This is Arles Struvie with a news update concerning the recently deceased Judge Roscoe Buckner, who died yesterday. Now the body was found by Nickey Mayberry, who'd come over to collect for the newspaper; Nickey wishes to squelch all rumors that the judge was found dead in a woman's bikini swimsuit. He says there's no truth to that rumor whatsoever.

THURSTON. (*On tape.*) It's not true.

ARLES. (*On tape.*) It's not.

THURSTON. (*On tape.*) It's not.

ARLES. (*On tape.*) It's not. It's not. According to Nickey, it was a 1950 turquoise, Dale Evans, one-piece swimming suit, with lots of cow-gal fringe. Services are pending at Hubert Funeral Home.

THURSTON. (*On tape.*) Ain't that awful? Ain't that awful?

ARLES. (*On tape.*) Gahhh!!

Scene Four: The Funeral Parlor

("In the Sweet By-and-By" plays. Lights come
up on funeral parlor,* **PEARL** *re-enters.)*

PEARL. Owww, Roscoe, is that you? What have they done to
you? My goodness, you look so waxy. Oh, they've waxed
you down so you'll look good...you old son-of-a-bitch.
A stroke! It was your conscience that killed you. Those
same tight little lips. Well, those beady little eyes will
never see the light again, will they, Judge? Oh, what
could have ever made me want to love you? Tell me,
how-how-how-how could I? I guess a young girl can be
foolish. But then you were always too good for me, now
weren't you, Judge? Just too good. That's all right. I
took it. But then you sent my favorite nephew, Stanley,
to reform school. And for what? Spray-painting stop
signs! Oh, Judge, you might as well have killed him.
He's never been the same. I told you then I'd sing over
your grave when you died... And Judge, I feel a song
comin' on!

OH, THE FOX WENT OUT ONE STORMY NIGHT.
HE PRAYED TO THE MOON TO GIVE HIM LIGHT.
HE SAID, "I GOT MANY A MILE TO GO BEFORE I
REACH THE TOWN-O, TOWN-O, TOWN-OOOOO..."*

*(***VERA CARP*** enters.)*

VERA. Why, Pearl Burras, is that you?

PEARL. Vera Carp, how are you?

VERA. *(Calling to the rear of the house to a non-appearing
son.)* Virgil, honey, wait out there in the lobby. Be
reverent.

(To **PEARL**.*)* Oh, I haven't seen you in so long.

PEARL. It's been a long time, Vera.

VERA. *(Referring to the judge.)* Isn't it awful.

PEARL. Doesn't he look lovely?

---

*Licensees should use melodies in the public domain for "In the Sweet
By-and-By" and "The Fox."

VERA. Well, I suppose.

    (To Virgil.) Virgil, I mean it.

PEARL. I think he makes a lovely looking corpse. Don't you think he looks nice?

VERA. Well, no, I don't.

    (To Virgil.) Virgil, that's to sign your name in, not to draw in. Quit it now!

    (To **PEARL**.*)* Well, Pearl, I just don't know what to say. One dead body just looks like another dead body to me. They just look dead and still and...

VERA & PEARL. Waxy.

VERA. *(To Virgil.)* Virgil, I'm gonna knock you into next week if you pick another flower! Go on. Go! Wait in the station wagon with Connie.

PEARL. Vera, that boy's not right.

VERA. *(After waiting out any audience laughter.)* Glass houses... Well, Pearl, Judge Buckner has met his maker at last.

        *(***VERA*** exits.)*

PEARL. In a Dale Evans swimsuit! Oh, Judge, I don't believe I can stand it!

    (She sings as she exits:)

OH THE FOX WENT OUT ONE STORMY NIGHT.
HE PRAYED TO THE MOON TO GIVE HIM LIGHT.
HE SAID, "I GOT MANY A MILE TO GO BEFORE I
REACH THE TOWN-O, TOWN-O, TOWN-OOOOOO."*

    *(***PEARL*** exits, changes to* **SPIKES**. *"When the Roll is Called Up Yonder" plays.** *Lights cross-fade to Coweta Baptist Church.)*

---

*Licensees should use melodies in the public domain for "The Fox" and "When the Roll is Called Up Yonder."

Scene Five: Coweta Baptist Church

(**VERA** *enters and addresses the audience:*)

VERA. Oh, Hi. How are you? Welcome to the Coweta Baptist Church, where everybody's welcome, even Catholics.

(To an audience member.) Hi; how are you? Isn't that a lovely outfit? I used to have one just like that…years ago. Isn't it wonderful how some people can just wear anything?

(To another audience member.) Why, I thought you were dead! I don't remember who told me that, but I'm so glad they were wrong. Hi. How are you? How are you? I, Vera Carp, vice president of the Smut Snatchers of the New Order, in the absence of our president, the Reverend Spikes, do hereby declare this meeting to be officially open. Now, we need to send out a communiqué from our education committee. Now after all the vicious things that have been said about us in the newspapers, we've decided to become more flexible on bilingual education. And we do indeed have a bilingual education program to submit to the Tuna schools. The difference is our program is one of moderation. It entails learning the following Spanish phrases. "Habla, usted, ingles?" which means "Do you speak English?"; "Cuanto?" which is "How much?"; Donde puedo cambiar este cheque?" which means "Where can I cash this traveler's check?"; "Por favor, envieme un botones para recoger mi equipaje," which is "Please send me a boy for my luggage," and the last one is "No he pedido esto," which is "I didn't order this!" Now that's all the Spanish any red-blooded American oughta feel obligated to learn. Now let's just see the newspapers make fun of that! …Well, he's still not here, so I'm gonna just forge ahead… We need to send out a snatch squad… Well, we do. We need to send out a book-snatchin' squad to the Tuna High School library to check the dictionaries. Now, we have a new list of

words that have been declared possibly offensive or misunderstandable to pre-college students. Now the words are: hot, hooker, coke, clap, deflower, ball, knocker, and nuts. Now after much prayer and soul-searching with the Lord, the committee has decided not to include the word "snatch" on the list. We know some of you have very strong feelings about "snatch." But we just can't afford to change our letterheads at this time.

(**REVEREND SPIKES** *enters.*)

Well, here he is. I hereby turn this meeting over to our honorable president, the Reverend Spikes.

SPIKES. Thank you, Vera. And folks, I'm so sorry I'm so late. But let's get down to business... Now, we're gonna send out a book-snatching squad to the Tuna High School library...

VERA. Oh, oh, oh. I already told 'em that.

SPIKES. Well, Vera, that's all the fun of being president is sending out the snatch artists.

VERA. I'm sorry. I won't do it again.

SPIKES. Please don't... All right, folks, we got a new communiqué on our bilingual education pro–

VERA. Oh, oh, oh. I already told 'em that, too.

SPIKES. Well, you just told 'em everything, didn't you?

VERA. Well, what did you expect 'em to do for fifteen minutes while you weren't here, sing show tunes?

SPIKES. Now, Vera, I'm not gonna get into this power struggle thing right here in front of all these people...

VERA. Hush...hush...the radio people are here.

SPIKES. Well, so they are. Hello, Arles, how are you? ...Fine, fine...how's that?

(*To* **VERA**.) Are we ready with the Buckner eulogy?

VERA. Of course.

SPIKES. Yes, we're ready with the Judge Buckner Eulogy. I'll tell you what, Arles, just set 'er up right back there. And when you're ready, just kinda wave your hand... Oh

– you're ready? All right... No, I'm ready... Okay... Are we live? ...This is the Reverend Spikes, and I just wanna say, I say I just wanna say a few words about a friend of mine and a friend of Tuna's. Judge Roscoe Buckner spent his whole life in service to his community, his country and his Lord.

(**VERA** *yawns.*)

And we're sure that when the roll is called up yonder, he'll be there. He was a judge who made hay while the sun shined...

(**VERA** *yawns again.*)

But always, I say always let a smile be his umbrella. He always kept his sunny side up and always saw the silver lining behind every cloud. A judge who took no wooden nickels, nor threw caution to the wind, but looked before he leapt and never got in over his head. No, he kept his head, when all about him were losin' theirs and blaming it on him. He kept a stiff upper lip and his nose to the wheel.

(**VERA** *begins to fall asleep.*)

About this man we can truly say he was one of a kind, a jolly good fellow which nobody can deny. He was one for all and all for one, and to his own self true. And I can tell you this, he did it his way. He was a serious-minded judge who let bygones be bygones, but remembered the Alamo. About this man we can truly say, he was the cream in Tuna's coffee. He fought fire with fire, and he kept the home fires burning. And when he couldn't stand the heat, he got out of the kitchen. He would walk that extra mile; he would walk it SOFTLY...

(**VERA** *wakes up.*)

And he'd carry a big stick. He was a Pepper, a man's man, early to bed, early to rise. He laid his cards on the table, gathered at the river and brought in the sheaves. Hunger was his best pickle...

VERA. What the devil does that mean?

(*VERA* exits, sharing her exasperation with the audience, and changes to *PETEY*.)

SPIKES. Hush, Vera. He was a judge who wouldn't fire until he saw the whites of their eyes, but whistled a happy little tune, praised God, and passed that ammunition, for he had not yet begun to fight. For never ever did I ever hear the man say die...he just did. He was a fine upstanding civil servant, who practiced what he preached, put his best foot forward and his money where his mouth was. And when the going got tough, he was gone. It's not easy to find the words to describe such a man, but I have done my best. We commend his soul to you, Lord. I, the Reverend Spikes, recommend him. Amen, Lord. Amen.

(*SPIKES* exits and changes to *BERTHA*. The tag to "When the Roll is Called Up Yonder" plays.*)

---

*Licensees should use a melody in the public domain for "When the Roll is Called Up Yonder."

Scene Six: The Greater Tuna Humane Society

(Lights cross-fade to the Humane Society. Music fades out to end. We hear **YIPPY** *barking off.)*

SPIKES AS YIPPY. *(Offstage.)* Yip. Yip.

*(***PETEY*** *enters.)*

PETEY. Listen.

SPIKES AS YIPPY. *(Offstage.)* Yip. Yip.

PETEY. Listen, here it is: "Any animal that can't be adopted within a reasonable amount of time must be destroyed at state expense. Destroying the animal is the only humane recourse." Now, Yippy, you can't say I haven't tried. You've been pet-of-the-week five times, and that's a record, and I'd love to keep you. But I got to stop somewhere. It's getting crowded here with the animals I already got... You stop it. Now I mean it, you just quit that... How can I put you out of your misery if you're wagging your tail?

(Pause.)

Come on. Come on, go on out there in the backyard and play.

SPIKES AS YIPPY. *(Offstage.)* Yip. Yip. Yip. Yip.

PETEY. Hey, hey, don't bark at Ruth. Snakes are very sensitive... I don't know if there's anybody up there. I never have understood much about religion, but if you are, I'd like to ask a few favors for the animals. Now I'm doing the best I can, but I've got over two dozen dogs, and I don't even have a count on the cats, and there's the ducks. Ever since the government flooded Buchner Basin, the wild ducks have got no nesting grounds left, so I'm up to my neck in homeless ducks. And it's tough being a duck. Cartoons portray ducks as genetic mutants with speech impediments. The very word "duck," when used as a verb means to rapidly lower your body position to avoid injury, so when you say "duck" to somebody, they don't know whether you're talkin' about a bird or an accident. And the Chinese eat their feet. And the other thing is huntin' season is just around the corner and that means the nightmares are gonna start again. Now after I hear the first shot, the nightmares start and they don't stop till November. I hate to bother you with it. I really do. But if you are up there and if you did create all this, we could sure use some help takin' care of it. Thank you. Amen.

　　*(**PETEY** exits and changes to **JODY**.)*

Scene Seven: Bertha's Kitchen ~ Christmas Eve

("Joy to the World" swells, then fades to radio.
Lights fade to radio. Music fades to radio test
tone, followed by* **THURSTON** *and* **ARLES** *on
tape. Lights gradually come up on Bertha's
kitchen;* **BERTHA**, *wearing a Christmas-
themed blouse, enters to continue baking and
decorating cookies.)*

ARLES. *(On tape.)* This is Radio Station OKKK in Tuna,
Texas, serving the Greater Tuna area at two hundred
and seventy-five watts signing on.

THURSTON. *(On tape.)* Merry Christmas, Tuna, this is
Thurston Wheelis.

ARLES. *(On tape.)* And this is Arles Struvie.

THURSTON. *(On tape.)* And this is the Wheelis...

ARLES. *(On tape.)* ...Struvie Happy Holiday Report. First
up, the Coweta Baptist Church in conjunction with the
Drop Back and Punt Club is conducting a twenty-four-
hour prayer vigil for Head Football Coach Raymond
Chassey as he tries for the third time to pass the Texas
State Teachers' Competency exam.

*(***BERTHA*** *thinks she hears something coming
from behind the pantry door.)*

THURSTON. *(On tape.)* If he flunks it again this time, he's
goin' into politics.

ARLES. *(On tape.)* That's right. So get down there to that
Coweta Baptist Church and pray, pray, pray!

*(***BERTHA*** *turns off radio, opens imaginary
pantry door. An imaginary cat hisses at her
from inside the pantry. She quickly shuts the
door, sighs, then re-opens the door. The cat
escapes and runs under the table.* ***BERTHA*** *goes
after it.)*

---

*Licensees should use a melody in the public domain for "Joy to the
World."

BERTHA. Kitty, kitty, kitty. Where did you come from, cat? How did you get in this house? What's wrong with you? *(Calling upstairs.)* Jody!

JODY. *(Offstage.)* What?

BERTHA. Get yourself down here pronto!
(Chasing the cat, calling after it.) Oh, no you don't! Get off of that! Jody!

     *(**JODY** enters and picks up the cat.)*

JODY. I guess you found the cat.

BERTHA. Is that what it is? I want it out of here, now.

JODY. Ah, Mama, she's gonna have babies.

BERTHA. Not here, she's not. And I don't have to ask you where you got it. Only Petey Fisk would dump a pregnant cat on me at Christmastime.

JODY. She doesn't have any place to go, Mama. Petey said all this cat needs is a warm blanket and some straw, just like in the manger.

     *(**JODY** exits into the pantry with the cat and changes to **ARLES**.)*

BERTHA. Jody, I am not playing midwife to some pregnant cat. I have too much to do today. I have a Smut Snatchers meeting at noon, I have a Frito pie to make for the radio station Christmas party, I'm supposed to be at Coach Chassey's prayer vigil, I haven't finished decorating these Christmas cookies, your father hasn't called and Stanley gets off probation tomorrow and the whole town thinks he's the Christmas Phantom.

JODY. *(Offstage.)* I know who the Phantom is.

BERTHA. And when your sister finds out we have a cat she'll have one herself. You know Charlene's allergic to cats!

JODY. *(Offstage.)* Maybe she'll pass out and we won't have to listen to her squawk.

BERTHA. Jody, if she does, I will make you hold her feet up till she comes to. That cat is going back to Petey Fisk today.

(Closes the door and calls upstairs.) Charlene Renee, Stanley Gene, get down here now or I'm going to put on the Andy Williams album!

JODY. *(Offstage.)* Mama, you promised last year not to play that record again.

BERTHA. *(Opening the imaginary pantry door.)* Honey, your father promised not to miss another Christmas. Hitler promised to stop after Czechoslovakia!

> *(***BERTHA** *slams the door shut.)*
>
> *(The telephone rings. She answers it.)*

Hello... Hello, Ike Thompson, nice of you to call back... Well, you may not want to wish me a Merry Christmas after you hear what I have to say... Yeah, yeah, listen, Ike. I want you to have my husband call his home... You don't know where he is, huh. Well, Ike, I suggest you finish your Christmas brew and get off your Christmas butt and go find him... Oh, I think you'll find him all right, 'cause if you don't the next message I leave will be with your wife, Ida. You remember Ida? And I'm telling her about that red-headed bank teller that my husband and you and half the men in this town play poker with in Sand City... Ike, now I'm already mad I had to leave a message at this nasty beer joint you're in. I'm sprayin' this phone down with Lysol when I hang up. And if I don't hear from my husband by this afternoon, I'm cashing in his poker chips and yours. Now you try to have a merry one. *(Hangs up.)* I'm a desperate woman.

> *(The doorbell rings; we hear barking.* **BERTHA** *answers the door.* **ARLES** *enters.)*

Get back, Woffie. Shut up! Come on in, Arles. I'm sorry; I think that just means he likes you.

ARLES. Well hell, if he liked me any better, we'd have to get married. That's a cute little dog you got out there, Bertha.

BERTHA. Well, Chiquita's a little hyper.

ARLES. Oh, I had one just like her when I was a kid – little ping-pong ball head, marble eyes, she shook a lot. We took her on vacation to Yellowstone and a hawk got her the first ten minutes.

BERTHA. Oh, Arles, that's terrible! Would you like a cup of coffee?

ARLES. Well, actually I came by to see Hank. Somebody turned his wallet in at the radio station.

(He takes out an imaginary wallet and places it on the table.)

BERTHA. Where did they find it?

ARLES. *(Pausing, uncomfortable.)* I can't say as I recall.

BERTHA. Oh, you can tell me, Arles; I'm used to Hank.

ARLES. Well, as I recall it was in a parking lot.

BERTHA. The parking lot of the Starlight Motel, wasn't it?

ARLES. Yeah. As I recall it was. I'm sorry.

BERTHA. Well, I appreciate you bringing it by.

ARLES. If it makes you feel any better I know just how you feel. My ex Trudy came home one time wearing Fruit-of-the-Looms.

(They both laugh.)

Well, I gotta run. I've got a lot of stuff to do before the party tonight. You come by the party if you feel like it.

BERTHA. I just might do that.

ARLES. Merry Christmas, Bertha.

*(**ARLES** exits and changes to **DIDI**.)*

BERTHA. Merry Christmas to you too, Arles. Lord, Christmas used to be so simple. Well, not always. I remember that Christmas Hank was in prison and I was workin' at the Tastee Kreme, cookin' on Christmas Eve, and that bread man from Odessa begged me to run away with him. He meant it, too. He'd been drinking but I know he meant it. Just where would you be now, Bertha? Well, I wouldn't have my babies and I wouldn't trade that for anything.

JODY. *(Offstage, makes the sound of a screeching cat.)* Mama! Mama!

BERTHA. *(Opening pantry door.)* Oh no, not now, cat. Please. It's all right, Jody. That's it, Miss Kitty, calm down. Nobody's going to bother you. Jody, reach up there and get that box down, honey. Hurry, we're going to need it.

> (**BERTHA** *exits, closing pantry door behind her. "Away in a Manger" swells* and fades to radio and out. Lights fade to radio and up on* **DIDI***'s spot.* **DIDI** *enters. She's smoking an imaginary cigarette.)*

DIDI. This is Didi Snavely asking you, do you know how dangerous it could be in this day and age to ride unarmed in a one-horse open sleigh? Well, lay your fears to rest, 'cause Didi's is stocked to the ceiling this Christmas with weaponry for the home, the car and the workplace. God forbid during this joyous season that anyone listening should become the victim of a Christmas theft. But wouldn't you rather shoot someone than watch them run off with your new toaster? I know I would. So whether it's a stun gun, judo clubs, or just a simple, old-fashioned switchblade, when you come to Didi's, you'll have a Holly, Jolly Christmas and the criminal will have a silent night.

> (**DIDI** *stubs out her cigarette on the floor and gets out another one as she exits.)*

---

*Licensees should use a melody in the public domain for "Away in a Manger."

Scene Eight: Didi's Used Weapons

*(Lights cross-fade to Didi's Used Weapons. A telephone rings. **DIDI** re-enters on the other side, lighting the cigarette.)*

DIDI.

GOOD KING WHAT'S-HIS NAME WENT DOWN...

(Picks up the phone.) Didi's Used Weapons. If we can't kill it, it's immortal... Hello, Dottie... Well, it's usually bad news when you call, Dottie. What's the matter, is your plane late or what? ...What do you mean, you're not comin'? ...Well, great. Why? ...Ah hell... Ah, hell... Ah, hell, he's always had that... Well, don't they have anti-fungal creams in California, Dottie? ...Well, you still gotta come get Mama... No. No. No, I had her last Christmas... I know you took her for Easter, Dottie. She's still got egg dye in her hair and under her nails and God knows where else. We can't even take her to church... Oh, yeah? Well, I've got a Christmas wish for you, too, Dottie. Yeah, well, I hope Santa craps down your chimney. *(Hangs up the phone.)* God, it is hell being a twin.

*(The cowbell rings and **BERTHA** enters. **DIDI** serves her coffee and they sit.)*

BERTHA. Hi, Didi. Are you busy?

DIDI. Come on in, Pickles, have a cup of coffee. I'm never too busy to chat with you.

BERTHA. Well, I thought you might be frazzled with the last-minute rush.

DIDI. Business is always brisk when the Phantom is on the loose. You be sure to thank Stanley for me.

BERTHA. I hope to God the cops don't catch him.

DIDI. Oh, Sheriff Givens couldn't catch a cold in the Klondike.

BERTHA. Well, Didi, I really stopped by to see if you have any burglar alarms left.

DIDI. I sold my last one yesterday. Are you having a problem with prowlers?

BERTHA. No, nothing like that. I just wanted something to wake me up when my worthless husband comes sneaking in late at night.

DIDI. Has Hank been out tom-cattin' again?

BERTHA. I tell you, Didi, it's hard to hold up when the whole town knows my husband's as useless as ice trays in hell.

DIDI. Don't get me started. R.R.'s been on a wandering binge lately. You know, Bertha, I often wonder how such well-brought-up girls like you and me could have married so bad.

BERTHA. It's a mystery.

DIDI. R.R.'s drinking has only gotten worse. He wanders off so much I decided I'd better find out something about safe sex.

BERTHA. *(Flustered.)* Oh, Didi! I swear!

DIDI. Can you imagine how depressed I got when I found out that's what we'd been doin' all along?

BERTHA. Well, I suppose some things are better left unknown.

DIDI. Amen, hallelujah.

BERTHA. Was that Ike Thompson I saw sneakin' away?

DIDI. Yeah. There's another one just as worthless as titties on a boar hog, but back to your Hank problem, I can order that burglar alarm for you.

BERTHA. No, that's all right, Didi. I'll just do what I've always done.

DIDI. What's that?

BERTHA. Rearrange all the furniture and unscrew all the light bulbs.

DIDI. Pickles, Pickles, Pickles. We sure knew what we were doing back in high school when we voted you the class wit.

BERTHA. Sometimes you have to laugh to keep from cryin'. Well, I gotta run. It'll take me a while to move that sofa. Merry Christmas, Didi.

DIDI. Merry Christmas, Bertha.

> *(We hear the cowbell as **BERTHA** exits. **DIDI** calls after her:)*

Don't strain your back.

(Exits singing.) Jingle Bells, Jingle... *(Takes a puff.)* ... the way...

> *(**DIDI** exits and changes to **ARLES**. "Jingle Bells" picks up where **DIDI** left off and plays on.* Music and lights fade to radio.)*

---

*Licensees should use a melody in the public domain for "Jingle Bells."

Scene Nine: Radio Station OKKK

(Lights come up on Radio Station OKKK.
ARLES *enters and turns off music by pushing*
a button on his desk.)

ARLES. This is Arles Struvie on Radio OKKK in Tuna, Texas. We're gonna be goin' off the air early tonight so we can have our annual Christmas party here at the station. Ever'body is invited to come on by, drop in, as long as you don't bring your kids, 'cause we don't want any fruit punch poured down our transmitters like last year. We'd like to take this time to thank our sponsors here at Radio OKKK, Clifford's Piano and Organ Shop over in Sand City. Clifford wants you to know it's never too late to get your hands on a good organ. So come by Clifford's, talk it over, and remember: at Clifford's they will hold your organ till Christmas. This is Radio Station OKKK in Tuna, Texas, signing off.

*(***ARLES*** *pushes another button. Radio lights*
go off. **BERTHA** *enters, carrying an imaginary*
Frito pie.)

BERTHA. Knock, knock.

ARLES. Well, come on in.

BERTHA. Well, am I the first one here?

ARLES. Yeah.

BERTHA. No matter how hard I try to make an entrance at a party, I'm always the first one through the door. I guess that's my destiny.

ARLES. Well, at least you get to see all the appetizers and Jell-O molds before folks eat 'em up.

*(***BERTHA*** *places her pie on an imaginary*
buffet table and looks over the buffet.)

BERTHA. Oh, there's a fancy one. What did she use to make the hooves?

(She takes a little taste, then picks up a buffet
plate and begins dishing up food. **ARLES** *takes*

*an imaginary record off a turntable, puts it
away in its sleeve, and returns it to a shelf.
He looks around and glances at his watch.)*

ARLES. I kinda wonder where ever'body is.

BERTHA. Well, I know Didi said she wasn't comin' because the party clashed with her TV schedule. She won't miss *Gunsmoke*.

ARLES. And Thurston went over to Sand City. Woolco had a special on bubble lights.

> **(ARLES** *samples one of the hors d'oeuvres as* **BERTHA** *pours herself a cup of punch.* **ARLES** *grimaces at the taste of the food and puts it back.)*

BERTHA. Well, I guess we shouldn't expect either one of them.

> *(There is a pause.* **BERTHA** *crosses to the table and sits.* **ARLES** *crosses to the punch bowl and pours himself a cup to wash away the bad taste.)*

ARLES. So, is your husband coming by?

BERTHA. I haven't even seen him today. Hank's not very good at parties. Besides he never was one for Christmas. Some of my worst memories of Hank are of Christmas.

ARLES. *(Crossing to the table to sit.)* You know, ol' Trudy could be the same way. She'd get meaner than hell right around Pearl Harbor Day and it could go all the way to Saint Patty's.

BERTHA. How long were you and Trudy married?

ARLES. Fourteen years.

BERTHA. That's a long time.

ARLES. Seemed like fifty. If we're gonna talk about Trudy I gotta have a snort.

> *(He takes out his flask and pours into his cup. He offers some to* **BERTHA**.*)*

You want some?

BERTHA. Oh, no. Thank you.

ARLES. Just a little snort in the punch?

BERTHA. No. It's against my religion.

ARLES. Well, who's gonna tell on ya?

BERTHA. I really couldn't.

ARLES. Well, if you really don't want any...

BERTHA. Well, maybe just one little shot in my punch. That's Maxie Bovine's punch. I recognize that.

ARLES. Um. Bitter.

BERTHA. Mm, that's much better. What were we talking about?

ARLES. How awful Christmas can be.

BERTHA. Oh, my. It used to be terrible when the kids were little. Hank would get drunk and put all the toys together the wrong way. Then he'd get mad and disappear. But the worst Christmas ever was the year Hank got out of prison and didn't bother to tell anybody. I spent all Christmas Eve on a bus to Huntsville and him not even there. Turnin' around comin' home on Christmas Day with nine-year-old twins fighting every inch of the way, and Jody was just a baby. And Lord, was it cold. Everybody had colds, the whole bus was hackin'. Then at a rest stop in Big Spring, Stanley talked Charlene into climbing into an empty luggage compartment. He locked her in and she screamed blue murder for ten solid minutes till I could find the bus driver to let her out. I'd have whipped them both had it not been Christmas. And it was cold.

> (**ARLES** *crosses to the punch bowl, taking* **BERTHA**'s *cup.*)

ARLES. Well, the worst Christmas I can remember was the year Trudy got mad and moved the trailer house one day while I was at work.

BERTHA. Why?

ARLES. Oh, hell, she was mad. She wanted an archery set for Christmas and I told her no.

> (**ARLES** *refills the cups.*)

BERTHA. Why did she want an archery set?

ARLES. I have no idea. Hell, our insurance was high enough because of her driving. I wasn't about to give her a bow and arrow.

BERTHA. And she moved the trailer?

ARLES. She moved it to New Mexico.

> (**ARLES** *crosses back to the table, handing* **BERTHA** *her cup on the way.*)

Just flat out ruined my Christmas.

BERTHA. I can imagine. Having your home disappear across state lines like that.

> (**ARLES** *pours a shot into his punch, then offers* **BERTHA** *one.*)

ARLES. You want another snort?

BERTHA. No, no, thank you.

ARLES. Just a little whiff in your punch?

BERTHA. I couldn't.

ARLES. A little dab'll do ya.

BERTHA. I mustn't.

ARLES. Well, if you really don't want any...

BERTHA. Well, just one more little shot.

> (*He pours just a little.*)

A little bigger than that.

> (*He pours her a healthier shot, to overflowing.*)

Oh, Arles!

ARLES. (*Pouring another for himself.*) And one for yours truly.

BERTHA. Well, it's a shame nobody else showed up for this party.

ARLES. It is, it is. I was hoping to get a little dancin' in.

BERTHA. Dancing? I didn't know there was gonna be any dancing. I probably shouldn't even be here. In my church we don't dance.

ARLES. You want another snort?

> (**BERTHA** *puts her glass forward.*)

BERTHA. Why not?

> (**ARLES** *pours a large shot for her.*)

You know one time in high school Vera and I sneaked over to Sand City and went to a dance. I let that slip one Saturday morning while Mama and I were cleaning the house and she whipped me with a vacuum cleaner hose.

ARLES. God Almighty!

BERTHA. Mama had a way of breakin' your bad habits. Every time I shampoo rugs I think about that time. And I've never been dancing since. I don't even remember how.

ARLES. *(Rises, tipsy.)* Well, I'll show you.

BERTHA. Oh, hush. I'm Baptist.

ARLES. *(Heading back to the punch bowl.)* Well, I am, too. But you know what? When I go out of town on business or conventions or stuff, I tell folks I'm a Methodist and I have one hell of a good time.

BERTHA. *(Presenting her empty cup to* **ARLES.***)* You are lying.

ARLES. *(Refilling the cups.)* No. One time we raised so much hell in Houston I claimed to be an Episcopalian.

BERTHA. What was that like?

ARLES. I don't remember too much about it. By the time I came to I was back in Tuna feelin' like a Baptist again.

> (**ARLES** *hands* **BERTHA** *her filled cup.*)

BERTHA. Episcopalian. Oh, my. I wouldn't have the nerve to do that, even for one night. Oh, Arles, it must be something, being a celebrity like you. You must have a lot of women after you.

ARLES. You'd think so, wouldn't you? But the truth is ever since ol' Trudy and I split the sheets I've kept every Saturday night open, but I always wind up playing Risk with Thurston or going over to Sand City with him for Chinese food.

BERTHA. No. A well-known broadcaster like you?

ARLES. It doesn't figure, does it? You know, I think the glare of the spotlight scares a lot of women off. And then Trudy said some mean things after the divorce, especially when the judge awarded me the trailer house. But hell, that trailer has been in my family for years.

BERTHA. It's practically an heirloom. The whole town knows that.

ARLES. But on the other hand, look at you, Bertha. I mean, sure, you've got your kids. But Hank? God Almighty! It makes me mad as hell to think that that worthless husband of yours has had a loyal, well-fed gal like you waiting at home for him all these years and he never took you dancing, not once.

BERTHA. I told you, Arles, we're Baptist.

ARLES. I don't care. Even Baptists oughta sin once in a while. That's what church is for. It's a place you go to feel better after you've done some sinning. It oughta make you mad as hell that man never took you dancing.

BERTHA. It's beginning to, the more I think about it.

ARLES. You want another snort?

BERTHA. Pour.

> (**BERTHA** *puts out her glass and* **ARLES** *pours her a drink. He swigs from the flask.*)

ARLES. (*After a moment.*) If I was Hank, I'd take you dancin' twice a week.

> (**BERTHA** *knocks her drink over on the table. She is flustered as she dabs the spill with an imaginary napkin.*)

BERTHA. Oh, Arles, I've spilled my drink. I really need to go now. I...

ARLES. Stop. Don't budge an inch.

BERTHA. What?

ARLES. It's the way them radio tube lights bounce off your bouffant.

BERTHA. My hair? Is there tinsel in my hair?

ARLES. Shhhh.

> (**ARLES** *moves to an imaginary stereo, picks out an album, places it on the turntable,*

and carefully puts on the needle. Texas slow-dance music starts to play. **ARLES** *hitches up his pants.* **BERTHA***, seeing this, gets up to go.)*

BERTHA. Arles, I'd better be goin' home now...

ARLES. Bertha, may I have this dance?

BERTHA. Well, Arles, I... I don't...

(Pause.)

Well, why not? I always wondered what it felt like to be a Methodist.

*(***BERTHA*** crosses to ***ARLES*** and they timidly start to circle slowly, not touching at first. ***ARLES*** puts his hands on ***BERTHA****'s waist and they begin to dance.* ***ARLES*** *indicates with a nod for* ***BERTHA*** *to put her hands on his shoulders. Finally,* ***ARLES*** *snuggles his head to* ***BERTHA****'s breast. When* ***BERTHA****'s back is turned to the audience,* ***ARLES*** *lets his hands drop to her rear end. He slowly turns her around and we see her eyes grow wide as the music swells and there is a blackout. Upbeat Texas music tags the scene.* ***BERTHA*** *and* ***ARLES*** *exit.)*

Intermission

ACT II

Scene One: Bertha's Kitchen
Fourth of July ~ 1990s

("Battle Hymn of the Republic" plays in the house.* Lights fade to radio as music fades to radio and segues into a radio test tone followed by **ARLES** *and* **THURSTON** *on tape.)*

ARLES. *(On tape.)* This is Radio Station OKKK in Tuna, Texas, serving the Greater Tuna area at 275 watts signing on.

THURSTON. *(On tape.)* Happy Birthday, America, this is Thurston Wheelis.

ARLES. *(On tape.)* And this is Arles Struvie.

THURSTON. *(On tape.)* And this is the Wheelis...

ARLES. *(On tape.)* ...Struvie Independence Day Report.

> *(Lights gradually come up on Bertha's kitchen.* **BERTHA** *enters, wearing a patriotic-themed blouse and begins making imaginary ice tea.)*

THURSTON. *(On tape.)* And first off in the news, the local chapter of the Smut Snatchers of the New Order has canceled all meetings until further notice according to Vera Carp, who serves as acting president any time the Reverend Spikes is under indictment or in rehab. It seems the Smut Snatchers have become a victim of their own success.

ARLES. *(On tape.)* They have.

---

*Licensees should use a melody in the public domain for "Battle Hymn of the Republic."

THURSTON. *(On tape.)* Yep, they sure have.

ARLES. *(On tape.)* I don't think they got rid of a library book since they went after *Black Beauty*.

THURSTON. *(On tape.)* What's wrong with *Black Beauty*?

ARLES. *(On tape.)* Vera says that it is chock-full of subliminal images.

THURSTON. *(On tape.)* Oh yeah. So, what are sub-lin-i-mal images?

ARLES. *(On tape.)* Hell if I know, but this is Texas, and we damn sure won't put up with them.

THURSTON. *(On tape.)* No, we won't

ARLES. *(On tape.)* We won't, we won't. Well, folks, on a personal note it's true that yours truly will be tying the knot tomorrow afternoon with my dearest baby, the widow Bertha Bumiller down at the home of W.H. and Vera Carp here in Tuna. Vera has requested that only close family be in attendance at the wedding due to the high quality of her carpets and the fact that too much in and out lets the house fill up with horse flies. We are registered for wedding gifts at Didi's Used Weapons here in Tuna.

     (**PETEY** *appears at Bertha's screen door.*)

PETEY. Hey, Bertha.

     (**BERTHA** *turns off the radio and lets him in.*)

BERTHA. Happy Fourth of July, Petey.

PETEY. I wanted to pay my condolences. I'm so sorry you had to put Woffie down.

BERTHA. I appreciate that, Petey. We waited as long as we could, hoping he would come around. But he was blind, deaf, and down to one good leg.

PETEY. Lord, that's worse than Didi Snavely's mother.

BERTHA. Almost.

PETEY. It must have been tough at the vet.

BERTHA. Well, yes and no. We took her to Lubbock to Dr. Fites, and Woffie was so far gone he didn't even try to bite him.

PETEY. Well, she was ready to go.

BERTHA. Oh yes. We buried her behind that holly bush but Shep dug her up and slung her all over the yard.

PETEY. That's a bird dog for you.

>   *(Pause.)*

So you're down to only six dogs.

BERTHA. What are you getting at?

PETEY. Well, I just thought...

BERTHA. Don't even start. Oh God, did you bring that box with you?

PETEY. Box?

BERTHA. On the porch.

PETEY. Well.

BERTHA. You've got a dog in that box.

PETEY. No, I don't.

BERTHA. Don't lie to me.

PETEY. I'm not.

BERTHA. I wasn't born in a blue state. Get that dog out of here.

PETEY. It's not a dog exactly.

BERTHA. Well, what exactly is it.

PETEY. Well, it started out as a cat.

BERTHA. You're talking like a spook.

PETEY. Let me finish. This little kitten turned up behind a liquor store in Lubbock and a friend brought him to me when he was three days old. His name is Pinkey.

BERTHA. I'm not taking a cat.

PETEY. He's not exactly a cat. Well, when Pinkey arrived I had this neurotic little Pomeranian named Cassie who had to be forced to nurse her own puppies. But mean as she was, she had a soft spot for Pinkey right off the bat and gave him all the milk he wanted. He became her favorite and turned out just like her.

BERTHA. What do you mean?

PETEY. He thinks he's a dog.

BERTHA. Shut up.

PETEY. He does. He bites tires, chews up slippers and guards the yard.

BERTHA. I don't believe that.

PETEY. I'm telling you, he's an attack cat. He'll keep the Amway salesmen beyond the gate, I'll tell you that.

BERTHA. You must think I'm crazy...

PETEY. Look Bertha, there's a couple of Jehovah Witnesses at the back gate right now.

BERTHA. Oh, God, nothing makes me madder than a so-called Christian that doesn't believe in war. Let it out of the box.

> (**PETEY** *steps outside, and after a moment the sound of a hostile cat is heard.* **PETEY** *exits and changes into* **ARLES**.)

Well, would you look at them leap that fence. I'll take the cat. What does he eat?

PETEY. (*Offstage.*) Any good dry dog food.

BERTHA. Don't worry; he'll have a good home here. Hey, Pinkey, stop digging in my flowerbed. Oh, look at him lifting his leg. He's so cute...

> (**BERTHA** *turns on the radio and we hear* **THURSTON** *on tape.* **BERTHA** *listens while she continues making a pitcher of instant ice tea.*)

THURSTON. (*On tape.*) This just in to the OKKK newsroom: Local militia leader Elmer Watkins and three followers have just taken Reba Childers hostage in her own home and they say they will not release her until the state government recognizes the northeast corner of Dewey County as the free and independent nation of Free White Texas. Reba, well-known wilderness scout and wife of local mayor Leonard Childers, has requested that everybody stay away and says she can handle the situation by herself. Folks, she's got that right. She could track a flea over concrete and bring down an elephant with an emery board on a sick day. The woman's deadly.

(**ARLES** *enters through screen door.*)

ARLES. Hey, baby.

(**BERTHA** *turns off radio.*)

BERTHA. Arles, come on in.

ARLES. It's nice and cool in here. I tell you I'm hotter than a pregnant mouse in a wool sock.

(*He kisses her cheek and sniffs the air.*)

Oh, you've done it again.

BERTHA. Done what?

ARLES. Give me another whiff.

BERTHA. Oh, my perfume. I forgot what effect Omaha Nights has on you.

ARLES. Don't you put it on again till after the wedding. A man can only take so much temptation.

BERTHA. Stop. You want some ice tea.

ARLES. Is it that instant with artificial lemon in it?

BERTHA. It sure is.

ARLES. I can't say no. I'm gonna stand over here by the air conditioner.

BERTHA. I tell you, Arles, if I had it to do over again, I would elope.

ARLES. I hear you, baby.

BERTHA. Vera is about to drive me crazy with all these details. You know how she can be.

ARLES. Well, you know, I've always liked Vera, but not very much.

BERTHA. Well, she's about to have a fit because I'm enjoying *Lonesome Dove*. I guess I'm going to have to read some more of the books we've banned. There's no telling what I've missed.

ARLES. That's the spirit.

BERTHA. Arles, you're so good for me. I enjoy life so much more with you in the picture. Here's your tea.

ARLES. Thank you, baby.

(*They drink.*)

ARLES. God bless whoever came up with instant tea.

BERTHA. I like it too.

ARLES. I got 'em.

BERTHA. Got what?

ARLES. Forty-eight-hour passes to the Rattlesnake Roundup.

BERTHA. Oh.

ARLES. Something wrong, baby?

BERTHA. Well, I've been meaning to bring that up, Arles. I really don't want to go there for our honeymoon.

ARLES. Why not?

BERTHA. Well, it's not very romantic, for one thing.

ARLES. Oh, you're going to love it.

BERTHA. Oh, Arles, let's go to Eureka Springs, Arkansas to the *Passion Play*. I've always wanted to.

ARLES. Talk about unromantic; that's not the kind of passion I had in mind.

BERTHA. Oh, it'll be great. We'll be up there in those cool mountains, and they say the play is wonderful. They have a new Jesus this year. He's a student from Texas A&M. Vera said he sent shivers down her spine.

ARLES. Baby, my mama dragged me to Sunday school for eighteen straight years. There's nothing you can tell me about Jesus.

BERTHA. Arles!

ARLES. Now, I'm bound and determined to have a better honeymoon than the one with Trudy. We went to Mount Saint Helens. God, what a flop that was.

BERTHA. I thought you weren't going to bring up Trudy. Well, my honeymoon wasn't any better. Hank took me to the drive-in movies in Del Rio.

ARLES. Hank. Hank. Hank.

BERTHA. The worst part was I'd already seen *I Spit on Your Grave, Part Two*. So, don't you see that's why I want to go to the *Passion Play*?

ARLES. Baby, I don't want to spend my honeymoon watching play-acting from the Bible.

BERTHA. Well, I don't want to have to check under my wedding bed for rattlesnakes.

ARLES. You got a stubborn streak, you know that? If everything doesn't go your way you get all huffy.

BERTHA. *(Getting huffy.)* When do I get all huffy?

ARLES. Well, you got all huffy over the wedding music and I gave in.

BERTHA. *(Huffy.)* I am not about to walk down the aisle to the tune of "Deep in the Heart of Texas." And I didn't say a word when you insisted on wearing cowboy boots to the ceremony.

ARLES. I've worn cowboy boots every day of my life, and I'll be wearing them in the great hereafter.

BERTHA. If you make it that far.

ARLES. I'll tell you one thing, if heaven has a dress code, I'll walk to hell in my Tony Lamas.

BERTHA. I hate it when you talk like that.

ARLES. Now you sound like your friend, Vera.

BERTHA. Let's don't fight. Here, you can help me fill out my reunion form while I work on this hangnail. Read the first line.

ARLES. Name. *(He writes.)* Bertha Struvie.

BERTHA. Better write Bumiller. I don't want to jinx us before the wedding.

ARLES. I'll just put Bertha. Everyone knows who you are.

BERTHA. That's what I love about small towns.

ARLES. Yeah, it's quaint.

BERTHA. You know, Arles, you fit in here so well, moving here from a big place like Sand City.

ARLES. It took a while, but you adjust.

BERTHA. How many in your senior class?

ARLES. There was a whole pack of us. Thirty-nine.

BERTHA. Oh, I'd feel all swallowed up in a crowd that big.

ARLES. One thing I'll say for it, it sure builds your social skills.

BERTHA. What's next on there?

ARLES. Any kids? Three. Profession?

BERTHA. Put Mother. That's tougher in my book than lion taming.

ARLES. Hobbies and pets.

BERTHA. Six dogs, oh and now there's Pinkey.

ARLES. Pinkey?

BERTHA. Our new cat

ARLES. (*Alarmed.*) Cat?

BERTHA. Petey Fisk brought him over today.

ARLES. Well, by God he can take it back. I hate cats.

BERTHA. You're just like my mama. She used to say cats were like politicians. They rub up to you and purr till they get what they want and then they go pee on the couch. But it's okay, Pinkey thinks he's a dog.

ARLES. Is this air conditioner on the blink?

BERTHA. No, why?

ARLES. Because you're talking like you had a stroke.

BERTHA. What?

ARLES. Well, something's wrong with your wiring if Petey Fisk has pawned a cat off on you claiming it thinks it's a dog.

BERTHA. Pinkey's stepmother was a Pomeranian. So he acts just like a dog.

ARLES. I don't care if he thinks he's a hula girl. I won't have a cat. Why, they can suck the breath right out of a baby.

BERTHA. Shut up, you sound like Charlene.

ARLES. Oh, I can assure you, I do not sound like Charlene. Don't worry. I'm gonna find that cat and take him back to Petey Fisk today.

BERTHA. I don't believe I would. Pinkey is an attack cat. You reach over the fence; you'll draw back a nub.

ARLES. Are you threatening me with your cat?

BERTHA. No. I'm just trying to save you a trip to the clinic. You ought to be grateful.

ARLES. (*Sarcastic.*) Oh, I am. And after we get back home from the *Passion Play*, I'll make me a little pallet under

the sink, and you can feed me soggy crackers every
morning.

BERTHA. Are you trashing my cooking?

ARLES. No, but first you want me to go see bathrobe Bible
stories on my honeymoon, and now I have to watch my
ass in case I'm being stalked by a rabid cat.

BERTHA. Watch your mouth.

ARLES. What?

BERTHA. Don't say ass around me, I'm a Christian.

ARLES. Ass, ass, ass, ass, ass.

BERTHA. You keep that up and you'll still be single this time
tomorrow.

ARLES. Are you threatening to divorce me before we even
get married?

BERTHA. What does it sound like?

ARLES. All right, by God it's off.

BERTHA. The wedding?

ARLES. I mean the whole damn outfit.

BERTHA. Well, that's fine with me. And you can wait out the
rest of tornado season in your trailer house, and I hope
you'll be real happy.

ARLES. And you can go to Arkansas to the *Passion Play* and
see how an Aggie comes off as Jesus.

(**ARLES** *exits and changes to* **DIDI.**)

BERTHA. *(After a long pause.)* Arles, you forgot to take your
ring. Oh well, I'll just put it in the mail.

(**BERTHA** *exits. Tag to "Battle Hymn of the
Republic" swells, then fades to radio.* Lights
fade to radio, then come up on **DIDI**'s *spot.* **DIDI**
enters, smoking an imaginary cigarette.)

DIDI. This is Didi Snavely reminding you on this national
holiday that fireworks make a pop, but a good firearm
makes a point. Now, when our nation's founders won

---

*Licensees should use a melody in the public domain for "Battle Hymn
of the Republic."

their independence from the ugly English, they didn't win it by invitin' them over for tea and crumpets. They won it because they shot 'em. And the English were obviously slow learners because they came back over here in 1812 and they shot 'em again. And they shot the Spanish at the turn of the century too. I don't remember why, but you know they had it coming. This country's freedom wasn't purchased with peace marches, protests, and EST seminars. We bought it with bullets, bombs, and bayonets. So come down to the store, demonstrate your commitment to the Second Amendment, and never forget that if our Texas forefathers had had bigger and better weaponry, it would be Mexico that remembers the Alamo.

(**DIDI** *stubs out her cigarette on the floor and gets out another one as she exits. Lights fade to radio, then cross-fade to Didi's Used Weapons.*)

Scene Two: Didi's Used Weapons

> (**DIDI** *re-enters on the other side, lighting the cigarette. She sings and smokes:*)

DIDI.

> OH SAY CAN YOU SEE BY THE DAWN'S EARLY...

> > (*She takes a long drag, singing the words in her head, then singing aloud with her exhale:*)

> LAST GLEAMING.

(She opens an imaginary door and calls in.) Mama, Mama, stop it! No! Put that out. We've been through this before. You can't smoke for thirty minutes after you've had ammunition in your mouth.

> (*Cowbell rings and* **BERTHA** *enters.*)

BERTHA. Hi, Didi.

DIDI. Pickles, I didn't hear you come in. I'm trying to break Mama from chewing on my shotgun shells.

BERTHA. Did that make her sick?

DIDI. No, she's fine, but I'll have to knock that merchandise down. They've got tooth marks all over them. What's wrong with you?

> (**DIDI** *gets* **BERTHA** *coffee. They sit and talk.*)

BERTHA. Promise not to tell.

DIDI. I promise.

BERTHA. It's off.

DIDI. Off?

BERTHA. The wedding. We broke off the engagement. I guess I didn't know him as well as I thought I did.

DIDI. Did he jilt you? Isn't that just like a man? Let me find you a good weapon.

BERTHA. No, Didi. I don't need a weapon.

DIDI. I don't mean kill him. I got weapons that are designed to maim.

BERTHA. I don't want to maim him either.

DIDI. No? Now what did I do with those little exploding booby traps? They scare the hell out of whoever sets them off. I put one on the shower curtain 'cause Mama hides in there during *America's Most Wanted*, but R.R. set it off.

BERTHA. Did it scare him?

DIDI. Hell, yes. When he wants to take a shower, he waits till dark and stands outside in the sprinkler. Did you and Arles have another fight about the wedding music?

BERTHA. No, no. We settled that. We're gonna let Vera decide. At least we were.

DIDI. Our song was "Sink the Bismarck." My kind of music.

(*Pause.*)

BERTHA. Funny how things change.

DIDI. Isn't it? Remember when R.R. first fell for me? How he'd follow me everywhere, wouldn't leave me alone? Back then it was infatuation. Today we'd call it stalking.

BERTHA. I loved Hank ever since that day in high school when they elected me FFA Sweetheart, and he drove me all over town on that John Deere tractor. I don't know when I stopped loving him, sometime after the twins were born, then he dropped dead when he found me dancing with Arles at that Christmas party, and now it looked like Arles was going to be perfect, but you know...

(**DIDI** *has lit a cigarette. The telephone rings.*)

DIDI. Damn it. Never fails. I light a cigarette, and before the smoke can hit my lungs, that damn thing rings.

BERTHA. If that's Arles, I'm not here.

DIDI. (*Answering the phone.*) Didi's Used Weapons. If we can't kill it, it's immortal... Yes, she's here, but she doesn't want to talk to you. Don't hem and haw with me. I know you've got another woman.

BERTHA. Didi...

DIDI. Let me tell you something you two-timing out-of-towner. You come in range of my rifle and I'll drop you like a flat beer. *(She hangs up.)* Pickles, I had no idea. Who is this Pinkey harlot?

　　*(***BERTHA*** giggles.)*

I know you're crying on the inside.

　　(Telephone rings.)

God...

　　(Telephone rings again.)

Damn it! *(She answers it.)* Hello. Hey, I told you not to call here. You better stay away from my friend unless your ass is bulletproof. *(She hangs up.)*

BERTHA. I gotta go, Didi.

DIDI. Stick around, Pickles. Maybe I can figure out a way to take out Arles and Vera Carp at the same time.

BERTHA. No, Didi, I appreciate it, I really do. I'm just going to go home and figure out what to do with all those wedding presents.

DIDI. Well, you know if there's any weaponry, I can always find a use for it.

BERTHA. Bye, Didi.

　　*(***BERTHA*** exits.)*

DIDI. Bye.

　　MY COUNTRY TIS OF THEE, SWEET...

　　(Takes a drag.)

...*THEE I SING*

　　*(***DIDI*** exits and changes to **ARLES**. Tag to "Battle Hymn" picks up where **DIDI** left off, swells in the house, then fades to radio.* Lights fade to radio. We hear **THURSTON** on tape.)*

THURSTON. *(On tape.)* This is Thurston Wheelis with a final update on that Free White Texas hostage crisis situation. Reba Childers had disarmed and tied up all three militia leaders who invaded her home earlier

---

*Licensees should use a melody in the public domain for "Battle Hymn of the Republic."

today and demanded a $400 fee for the release of her hostages to cover rug damage, or she said she would kill them. And we have confirmed that the organization was able to raise $375 and promised Reba to deliver the other twenty-five as soon as the bank opens tomorrow morning. Services are pending at Hubert Funeral Home.

Scene Three: The Starlight Motel

(Lights cross-fade from radio to the honeymoon suite of the Starlight Motel. Slow Texas dance music plays.* ARLES enters and arranges the chairs into a bed. BERTHA enters and they stand on either side of the bed. Music fades.)

BERTHA. Well, here we are.

ARLES. Yep, here we are.

(Pause.)

Right here.

BERTHA. Arles, thank you for the flowers. I'm so glad you could find some on such short notice. I just wouldn't feel like a bride without flowers.

ARLES. It's a good thing that grocery store was open. You have to think fast when you elope.

BERTHA. And the Justice of the Peace and his wife were so nice.

ARLES. She sure could play that accordion.

BERTHA. Oh, my, yes. She went to town on that accordion.

ARLES. And I thought their kids lighting those sparklers as we left was a nice touch.

BERTHA. Oh, and Arles, thank you for going by the car wash and getting all that writing off the back window. What was it they wrote back there?

ARLES. They said, "It'll be a hot time in the old gown tonight."

BERTHA. Lord, I hope nobody noticed that.

ARLES. I don't think so. The whole town was out at the stockyards watching the fireworks.

(Pause. They sit on the bed.)

---

*A license to produce *Deep in the Heart of Tuna* does not include a performance license for any third-party or copyrighted music. Licensees should create an original composition or use music in the public domain. For further information, please see Music Use Note on page 3.

BERTHA. Well, here we are.

ARLES. Yeah. Here we are.

(Pause. He pats the bed.)

Nice firm mattress.

BERTHA. Uh-huh. Nice and firm.

(She gently bounces on the bed.)

I don't like them too firm.

ARLES. *(Overlapping.)* I like 'em real firm.
(To **BERTHA**'s *comment.)* You don't?

BERTHA. Oh, this one is fine, just fine.

ARLES. I can call the desk and have them bring another.

BERTHA. No, no.

ARLES. You know what the desk clerk said about satisfaction being guaranteed. I can help him bring in another mattress if that's what you want.

BERTHA. I wouldn't think of it. This one is just fine. Nice and firm.

ARLES. Firm.

(Pause.)

BERTHA. Pretty wallpaper.

ARLES. Uh-huh.

(Pause.)

Real pretty.

BERTHA. I like yellow.

ARLES. Goes good with your hair.

BERTHA. Thank you.

(She looks up at the ceiling.)

What is that hanging from the ceiling?

ARLES. I expect those bolts used to hold a mirror up there.

BERTHA. A mirror? Why would anybody hang a mirror above a bed?

ARLES. Well, it is a honeymoon suite.

BERTHA. *(Thinks for a moment, then gets it.)* Oh, my, I could never watch that. I'd have to wear sunglasses or something. I'd be worried to death it would fall.

ARLES. *(Laughs.)* Well, that's not the way like I'd like to be found, sandwiched between my bride and a two-hundred-pound mirror.

> *(They both laugh. There is a pause.* **BERTHA** *reaches over to an imaginary nightstand, takes a pill, and washes it down with water.)*

That's not a hormone pill, is it?

BERTHA. *(Surprised.)* No. It's for my acid reflux.

ARLES. Thank God Almighty. I want you to promise me something.

BERTHA. What?

ARLES. If the doctor ever puts you on hormones, I want you to promise to tell me and for God sakes promise to take them.

BERTHA. Why?

ARLES. Just promise, I've travelled this route before.

BERTHA. All right, I promise.

ARLES. Trudy used to get mad and refused to take her hormones.

BERTHA. Did that make her mean?

ARLES. Mean? Mean with back hair. It got so bad when she refused to take 'em, hell, I'd take 'em instead.

BERTHA. Arles!

ARLES. Hell, one of us had to have some relief.

BERTHA. Did they affect you?

ARLES. I didn't notice much change. I started going to a lot of Julia Roberts's movies.

> *(He laughs, she doesn't.)*

That's a joke.

BERTHA. I don't get it.

ARLES. Let's just let it pass.

(There is a pause. **BERTHA** *hiccups.)*

ARLES. Are you all right?

BERTHA. This happens whenever I get nervous. *(Hiccups.)*

ARLES. Can I do anything for you?

BERTHA. Distract me. If I put my mind on something else it will stop. *(Hiccups.)*

ARLES. Okay.

> *(He searches for a subject.)*

Nice big TV.

> *(***BERTHA*** *hiccups.)*

Two hundred channels. You want me to turn it on?

BERTHA. No, I'm fine. *(Hiccups.)*

ARLES. We can find out about the weather in Arkansas, see what it's going to be like when we get there.

BERTHA. No, I'd rather be surprised. *(Hiccups.)* Thank you, Arles, for agreeing to take me to Eureka Springs. I know you'll like it.

ARLES. I just want you to be happy, baby.

> *(***BERTHA*** *hiccups.* ***ARLES*** *puts his hand behind her and touches her. She screams.)*

I'm sorry.

BERTHA. Oh, that scared me.

ARLES. Why?

BERTHA. Well, I didn't know who it was.

ARLES. Nobody here but us chickens. *(Laughs.)* That's another joke.

BERTHA. I don't get that one either.

ARLES. Well, it's not supposed to be comedy night at the Grand Ole Opry. It's supposed to be a wedding bed.

BERTHA. Well, excuse me, but it's been a long time since I've been in a wedding bed.

ARLES. Well, it's not something I'd think you'd forget. It's like riding a bicycle.

BERTHA. I never got the hang of a bicycle.

ARLES. Great.

BERTHA. Arles, don't get mouthy with me.

ARLES. I'm not getting mouthy with you. All I did was touch you.

BERTHA. And I told you I didn't know who it was.

ARLES. Who in the hell did you think it was?
(Looks under the bed and yells.) All right, everybody out!

BERTHA. That's not funny.

ARLES. I couldn't agree more.

> *(Pause.)*

Well, we might as well see what's on the tube.

BERTHA. Don't you dare. I'm not spending my honeymoon watching television commercials.

ARLES. Well what would you like to do? I've got a frisbee in the car.

BERTHA. I'm sorry, Arles. I'm nervous because I want it to be beautiful this time. I was so infatuated with Hank, and he treated me like a retread. I spent my whole life waiting on that man, waiting for him to get home from work, waiting for him to show up at the hospital when the twins were born, which he never did, waiting for him to get out of prison.

ARLES. You know, one time I waited three months for Trudy to come home from the grocery store. She left one night to get cigarettes, said she'd be back in ten minutes, and it took me three months to find her.

BERTHA. Where'd you find her?

ARLES. Playing bingo on an Indian reservation in Oklahoma.

BERTHA. Oh, my. What did she say when you found her?

ARLES. She asked me for a cigarette.

BERTHA. Oh.

ARLES. We never did find the car.

BERTHA. Well, we both deserve better. I think this new marriage should offer us something different, don't you agree?

ARLES. One hundred percent. And I've got just what we need right here. *(Pulls out a book.)*

BERTHA. What is it?

ARLES. It's a book about healthy sexual relationships between a husband and wife that I got from my cousin Slim.

BERTHA. The preacher?

ARLES. Yep.

BERTHA. Let me see that.

> *(She takes the book and starts leafing through it.)*

Would you look at the size of that word. It's too big for *Wheel of Fortune*.

ARLES. Read what it says there.

> (**BERTHA** *reads.*)

BERTHA. Oh, I could never do that.

ARLES. Why not?

BERTHA. Well, I'd get the giggles, for one thing.

ARLES. Read at the top of the next page.

BERTHA. *(Reads.)* Well I don't... That's just... Have you ever done that?

ARLES. Well...

BERTHA. Arles!

ARLES. Read on.

BERTHA. *(Reads.)* And you got this from a preacher?

ARLES. There's nothing in there that's not part of a healthy sexual relationship between a husband and wife.

BERTHA. I don't know.

ARLES. Turn the page.

BERTHA. *(Turns the page and is totally shocked.)* Oh Lord, how did they manage that?

> *(She hands the book to* **ARLES**.*)*

I've seen enough. I had no idea folks did that sort of thing.

ARLES. All the time.

BERTHA. And to think all these years I was married to a man whose bedroom manner was roll over and play dead. Why that sorry son-of...

ARLES. Baby, Hank and Trudy are part of the past, and every time we bring them up, we go back there. We don't need to do that. We've got everything ahead of us. I promise you, this marriage is going to be different.

BERTHA. Well, all right. But if I'm going to do that... *(Indicates a place in the book.)* ...then you need to get things rolling like it shows on page seventeen.

ARLES. *(Finds page seventeen.)* I think I can oblige you.

BERTHA. My pleasures are important, too.

ARLES. I hear you, baby.

BERTHA. I want to feel desired.

ARLES. Don't hold back.

BERTHA. And never taken for granted.

ARLES. Baby, baby, baby.

BERTHA. I want to be pursued.

ARLES. You want to be pursued?

BERTHA. I want to be pursued by you, and only you.

ARLES. You want to be pursued?

BERTHA. I want to be pursued.

　　　　(Short pause.)

ARLES. *(Gets out of bed.)* Well, take off.

　　　　(ARLES *tickles* **BERTHA** *and she gets out of bed. She runs a few steps. He chases her around the bed, first one way, then the other.)*

BERTHA. Arles, stop it. You are so silly. Arles, you're going to make me pee in my pants.

ARLES. Don't fight it, baby. It's bigger than the both of us.

　　　　(BERTHA *and* **ARLES** *disappear. We see parts of their clothing thrown onto the stage.* **BERTHA** *enters with* **ARLES** *in pursuit, his pants down around his ankles. They disappear again.* **ARLES** *runs in as if being chased, looks back.* **BERTHA** *enters, scantily clad, makes a provocative pose, and chases* **ARLES** *off. Party music and lights fade to radio as lights come up on* **DIDI**'s *spot.* **DIDI** *enters, smoking.)*

DIDI. This is Didi Snavely asking you, are you tired of wasting time and money on anti-depressants and expensive doctor visits? Well come by the store and elevate your mood the cheap and easy way with a good old used weapon from Didi's. For that low-life burglar sneaking in an unlocked window, how about our petite, mother-of-pearl, inlaid snub-nose? I call it the Sweet Sue; it's compact, decorative and deadly through double-pane glass. Or if it's animals you're after, our Bambi Maker sure-shot deer rifle is perfect for most large game and the occasional drunk, belligerent hunter. Buy two, and we'll throw in that gun rack for half-price. So come by the store, scratch that itchy trigger finger, and remember what we always say at Didi's: Don't just hang up on telemarketers, track 'em down and shoot 'em.

> (**DIDI** *stubs out her cigarette, exits, changes to* **ARLES**. *Texas Valentine music plays.* *Lights and sound fade to radio.*)

Scene Four: Bertha and Arles' Kitchen
Valentine's Day ~ 2000s

(Lights come up on Bertha's kitchen. **BERTHA** *enters, wearing a Valentine's Day-themed blouse.* **ARLES** *enters. His mustache has become grey. He sees* **BERTHA** *and sneaks up behind her.)*

ARLES. *(Grabbing* **BERTHA** *from behind.)* Gotcha!

BERTHA. Ahhhhh!! Arles, you scared me. Lord, what will the neighbors think hearing me scream like that?

> *(***BERTHA** *turns off radio.)*

ARLES. Well, they better think fast, 'cause we'll be outta town by noon and they'll be left to snoop on each other.

BERTHA. Still, I don't want them hearing me scream like a banshee.

ARLES. That's why you're gonna like Las Vegas. Why, there's a strange sound coming behind every closed door, and nobody even bats an eye.

> *(***ARLES** *fixes himself an imaginary cocktail.)*

BERTHA. Really? Even on Sundays?

ARLES. Yep.

BERTHA. Well, I just hope we're doing the right thing spending all this money renewing our wedding vows.

ARLES. Well, we can't back out now. I'll never get the deposit back.

BERTHA. And I feel all strange not having any bridesmaids or family.

ARLES. We didn't have any last time, remember? We eloped. Besides, here they got a bridesmaid on call. They throw her in for an extra fifty.

BERTHA. Damn, that's a lot of money.

ARLES. You're worth it, baby, ever nickel. Just think, this time tomorrow you'll be slopping on suntan lotion by the pool at the Hula Chateaux Resort.

BERTHA. Oh, Arles, I can't be traipsing around the hotel in a swimsuit. Somebody might see me.

ARLES. Baby, we don't know a soul in Las Vegas. What do you care if somebody sees you?

BERTHA. I suppose you're right. Why should I worry about what some stranger from Nebraska thinks about me no matter how sophisticated they might be, and Pearl gave me her floral swimsuit. She said she was too big to go swimming. She claimed boats tried to tie up to her.

ARLES. Your Aunt Pearl is funny as a crutch.

BERTHA. But Arles, you know how shy I am, have been my whole life. It got so bad when I was a teenager I had to shower in the dark.

ARLES. Baby, we're going to get that swimsuit wet if I have to spread a tarp out in the hotel room and go at you with a squirt gun.

BERTHA. That's nasty.

ARLES. Come on, baby, we're going to the Liberace museum.

BERTHA. Oh, you changed your mind.

ARLES. I'll buy you all the shrimp scampi you can wolf down.

BERTHA. You know I love shrimp scampi.

ARLES. We'll knock back Mai Tais and save those little umbrellas.

BERTHA. For my collection.

ARLES. Come on now. Baby, just think, five whole days in a place where you can have Venice without the pigeons, New York without the Yankees, and Paris without the French, how good can it get?

BERTHA. All right, come on let's go dig out that ol' nasty swimsuit.

ARLES. Baby, baby, baby!

BERTHA. Happy Valentine's Day.

(**BERTHA** *and* **ARLES** *exit.*)

Scene Five: Bertha and Arles' Kitchen
Three Days Later

(Vegas music starts up lively, then grinds to a halt. Lights fade out and back up on Bertha and Arles' kitchen, now at night. **ARLES** enters in a bad mood and wearing a t-shirt and pajama bottoms with his cowboy hat. He crosses to kitchen counter and fixes himself a drink.)*

ARLES. Well I'll tell you, it's a hell of a note when you have to leave from your second honeymoon three days early.

> *(**BERTHA** enters, wearing a robe, to continue unpacking an imaginary suitcase. They're both in bad moods, miffed at one another.)*

BERTHA. Well, I'm almost unpacked, just one more bag. What is this?

ARLES. What?

BERTHA. This orange plastic thing.

ARLES. I told you I was going to spread out a tarp in the hotel room and squirt you with a water pistol if that's what it took to get you in that swimsuit. The squirt gun's in there somewhere. You were so upset about that vibrating bed; I thought I better not bring it up.

BERTHA. Don't bring it up. I never heard of such a thing, dropping a quarter into a slot and the bed starts shaking like a faith healer.

ARLES. It said on the thing that bed emitted a soothing calming vibration.

BERTHA. That was a lie. It knocked pictures off the wall. That's as close to an earthquake as I intend to get. I've still got a charley horse from hiding in that bathtub.

---

*A license to produce *Deep in the Heart of Tuna* does not include a performance license for any third-party or copyrighted music. Licensees should create an original composition or use music in the public domain. For further information, please see Music Use Note on page 3.

ARLES. I didn't scare you on purpose. I know how you are about that.

BERTHA. I'll get you back, and it'll be worse than last time.

ARLES. What could be worse than flipping off the lights while I'm taking a shower and putting on the music to *Psycho*? I've been taking tub baths for six months.

BERTHA. You knew better than to sneak up behind me and kiss me on the neck when I'm watching a vampire movie.

ARLES. I wasn't sneaking.

BERTHA. If I don't hear you, it's sneaking.

ARLES. Well, what am I supposed to do when I feel a little frisky, put on some wooden shoes?

BERTHA. You'll know it when I get you back.

ARLES. You didn't even try to have a good time. You wouldn't even get out of the room.

BERTHA. I counted three rattlesnakes in the parking lot.

ARLES. We have rattlesnakes here in Tuna.

BERTHA. Those are our rattlesnakes; they're used to us. I saw one by the porch when we came in. Lord, I hope Jody remembered to lock the back door after he fed Hop-Sing. What a flat tire of a vacation.

ARLES. Don't blame me. I wanted to rent a car and go see that big dam.

BERTHA. I've seen a dam and a lake before.

ARLES. Where?

BERTHA. Lubbock.

ARLES. Oh well, we've been to Lubbock; there's nothing left to do but just lay down and die.

> *(He pours another shot into his drink.)*

And we had to leave early. How could we stay if you wouldn't get near the bed? Happy Valentine's Day.

> *(He lifts his glass in a mock toast. Thinks better of it and empties his drink in the sink.)*

BERTHA. I was afraid the bed would come back on again.

ARLES. Baby, you heard the noise that bed made when it shorted out, it sounded like a milk cow choking on a soccer ball. There's only one thing in the world that could come back after making that kind of sound.

BERTHA. What?

ARLES. Cher.

> *(They both laugh. **ARLES** gets punch from fridge and pours a glass.)*

You want some punch?

BERTHA. Yes I'll have some punch. Well, I'm glad it's over and we're home. I was so tired of everybody being nice to us.

ARLES. Me too. I don't know what got into 'em.

> *(He pours another glass of punch.)*

BERTHA. Oh God, Arles, there's a snake on the floor!

ARLES. *(Jumping up on a chair.)* God Almighty, call the sheriff! Where's Petey Fisk?

BERTHA. I told you I'd get you back.

ARLES. Well, I'm so glad that's out of the way. Okay, we're even. Come sit down here beside me.

BERTHA. Well, I guess we should just chalk up Las Vegas to experience, but I still think we could have saved some time and gotten that fortune teller to help us out. I wasn't really going to believe her. I just wanted to experience something new and fun and to do it with you.

ARLES. Well, baby. Tell you what, you look in the Lubbock paper in the want-ad section. I've seen a bunch of fortune tellers in there, so you pick one and I'll drive you over there and we'll see what they have to say.

BERTHA. Really? You'll pay for a full session?

ARLES. And after we'll go to that Mexican place on the wrong side of town and get some enchiladas.

BERTHA. I know just the lady.

> *(Pause. She sits beside him.)*

BERTHA. Lord, I'm so tired. I hoped this whole idea was going to be a real picker-upper till I saw that tattooed bridesmaid. I don't think Bob Hope could have made her laugh. Lord, she was sulky.

ARLES. And Itchy.

BERTHA. You noticed that, too. I wasn't about to walk down the aisle with a bridesmaid scratching like a bird dog.

ARLES. Well, we've done it.

BERTHA. What?

ARLES. All that talk about itching and scratching and I get this place. *(Indicates his back.)* Get it for me, would you?

BERTHA. Oh.

(She scratches his back.)

ARLES. Lower... A little to the left... All right. Now pop the clutch. Ahhhhhhh! If I could get you to talk dirty when you do that, we'd have the best marriage in Texas.

BERTHA. *(Playfully slaps him.)* We already do.

ARLES. Oh, thank you baby.

BERTHA. Can you tell me something? Why did we feel the need to spend all that money to go someplace to be alone together? We can do that right here. I mean we don't have a big fountain that dances to movie music. But, remember that winter when Buford Posey ran over the water main and it all froze over? Joe Bob brought all the cast of *Christmas Carol*, and they all sang "Winter Wonderland." Las Vegas doesn't have anything like that.

ARLES. And not likely to any time soon. And you know all that talk about the bright lights out there? They don't hold nothing to the night that lightning hit Cooter Wooten's windmill forty-two times in twenty-eight minutes.

BERTHA. Yeah. Melted that metal rooster up on top.

ARLES. Sure as hell did. Remember how she wandered the streets mumbling, "I'm a sinner. God fried my chicken."

BERTHA. And she still has that tick?

ARLES. Oh, she goes off like a coo-coo clock when it rains.

BERTHA. And if we are ever going to renew our vows, I want to do it in our own church, right here in Tuna.

ARLES. With Reverend Sominex?

BERTHA. Be nice. Reverend Merkel is a fine young preacher and he's bound to get better with time.

ARLES. He's fine by me. Hadn't woke me up once.

BERTHA. I should slap you.

ARLES. You're so full of promises.

BERTHA. You know I only saw one church in Las Vegas, and it was catty-cornered to Hooters. That is the last thing I want to see after Sunday services, a big sign that says "Hooters."

ARLES. That might inspire some impure thoughts and speaking of which, I'm still bent out of gear we never got you in that swimsuit.

BERTHA. I know. I was looking forward to sitting by the pool with you and maybe even getting in, but I just know I can't do that. I blame my mama. She was so Baptist about everything. She always made me wear a swimsuit that was so loose, I made bubbles every time I got in the water. Embarrassed me to death.

ARLES. You need to get some professional help with that "Mama" stuff. Mine messed me up, too.

BERTHA. How so?

ARLES. Well, you knew my mama wrote the Bible.

BERTHA. Stop it.

ARLES. She did. She'd pray over anything. It was nothing to walk into the kitchen, and there'd be Mama praying and laying hands on a broken coffee percolator.

BERTHA. Did it work?

ARLES. No, Daddy would fix the short later, and nobody would tell her.

BERTHA. Your mama was nice.

ARLES. Nice, my...foot. She nicknamed me Runt, told the neighbors I was too little to matter much. That's why I played high school football. I'd climb into a big old pile of bodies and grab some old boy by the lips and try to pull them off his head, and I thought about Mama the whole damn time.

BERTHA. People talk about Texas men, but it's really the Texas women who do the real damage.

ARLES. Oh, hell yes.

BERTHA. Well, Arles, I did some thinking on that long plane ride home and I made some decisions about Mama and about us, and I've decided I'm going to quit being afraid and worrying about Mama or the neighbors or the TV preachers and to enjoy life like I've got a right to, and I don't have to run off to Las Vegas to do it.

ARLES. What are you driving at?

BERTHA. Now don't interrupt me till I'm finished.

> *(She goes to the window and pulls the curtains tight.)*

First of all, tonight... Well, tonight... Well, tonight, I want you to leave the lights on.

ARLES. You mean, when we... Oh, baby!

BERTHA. I'm not finished. I've got something else to show you. Well...about that swimsuit.

> **(BERTHA** *turns her back to the audience and opens up her robe to* **ARLES.)**

Happy Valentine's Day.

ARLES. *(Whistles.)* Oh, baby, baby, baby.

BERTHA. *(Closing her robe.)* Well, come on. Get up and help me.

ARLES. Get up? Why?

BERTHA. I need some help with this plastic sheet.

> **(BERTHA** *takes out the imaginary tarp from the suitcase and hands it to* **ARLES.** *He spreads it on the floor.* **BERTHA** *takes out the water pistol from the suitcase.)*

Squirt squirt.

(**BERTHA** *gives* **ARLES** *the water pistol, turns her back to the audience, and opens her robe.* **ARLES** *squirts her from different angles.)*

Not the hair!

(They are both giggling.)

Not-there-not-there-not-there. Oh, that's cold! Oh, Arles! Stop! Oh, Arles, you're such a bad boy!

(**BERTHA** *chases* **ARLES** *off, letting her robe slip down and reveal her swimsuit. They exit as Texas party music comes up.**)

End of Play

---

*A license to produce *Deep in the Heart of Tuna* does not include a performance license for any third-party or copyrighted music. Licensees should create an original composition or use music in the public domain. For further information, please see Music Use Note on page 3.